KITTEI

Snowflake

Lynne Dennis

Carnival

Snowflake wakes up.

"Where am I?" she thinks sleepily.

"I want to get down, Pickle," she says.
"Easy," says Snooze.
But Snowflake is not sure.

All the other kittens jump down.
"Wait for me," says Snowflake.
Snowflake climbs up
instead of jumping down.

"What's in here?" thinks Pickle.
She pushes open the door.

Poor Snowflake. She clings on tightly.

A jug rolls out of the cupboard.
"I'll jump onto that," thinks Snowflake.

Hop and Scotch climb in
and out of the shelves.

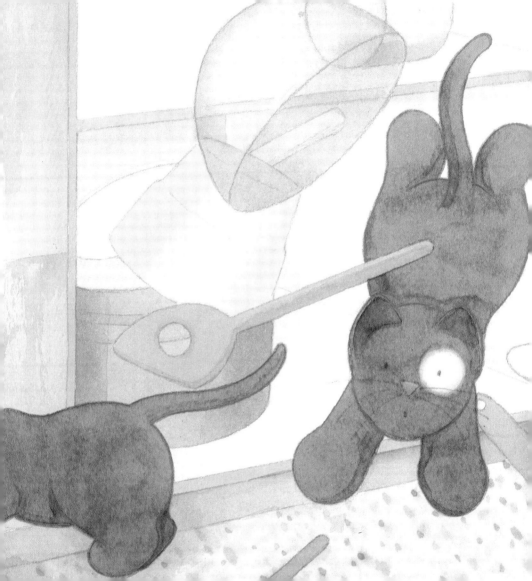

Bang! Crash! Hop falls down.
So do the dishes!

What's that?
One of the bowls is moving.
"'It's got a tail," says Scotch.

Out pops Snowflake.
"Time for a drink," she says.